THIS BOOK BELONGS TO:

SECRET IDENTITY

Do not fill this bit in or
Dr Septic will know who you are
....

SUPERHERO NAME

....

JOHNNY CATBISCUIT

AND THE ABOMINABLE SNOTMEN!

MICHAEL COX

ILLUSTRATED BY GARY DUNN

EGMONT

To Jo, Tom and Edie

EGMONT

We bring stories to life

Johnny Catbiscuit and the Abominable Snotmen!
First published in Great Britain 2008
by Egmont UK Limited
239 Kensington High Street
London W8 6SA

ISBN 978 1 4052 3737 6

1 3 5 7 9 10 8 6 4 2

A CIP catalogue record for this title is available from the British Library

Printed and bound in Great Britain by the CPI Group

CONTENTS

PROLOGUE

The film was very jumpy and blurred, with poor sound quality. But what Johnny Catbiscuit and Felix Pawson saw and heard made their blood run cold. It opened with a shot of the woods, taken through the cottage window. Roaming through the trees was a huge creature, like nothing they'd seen before. It looked part-bear, part-baboon. But with a hideous, human face! Apart from its truly fearsome facial features, it was covered from head

to toe in shaggy white fur. But, most appalling of all, were the torrents of thick, green snot, which oozed and bubbled from its horrid, pear-shaped nose. A positive Niagara of extremely wet and lumpy hooter-goo gushed from its cavernous nostrils, then fell in great blobs on the snow, where it frothed and steamed and sizzled, almost as if it had a life of its own!

The gruesome creature now spotted the cottage and lumbered towards it. Moments later there was a crash and the massive beast was silhouetted in the doorway. Now, the person holding the camera began moving through the house, their shots becoming fitful and confused.

Nevertheless, despite obviously being terrified out of their wits, they kept on filming.

'It's chasing them!' said Johnny, through gritted teeth.

Next came a series of jerky, random shots of the kitchen, followed by garden, snow and sky. There were muffled screams, yelps and roars. Now there was a close-up of teeth and claws. Then the screen went blank.

'That poor person!' gasped Johnny. 'How they must have suffered!'

'And that monster!' groaned Felix. 'Whatever could it be?'

'I don't know,' said Johnny. 'But I know

3

someone who might!' He flipped his wrist-pod into 'Communicate' mode, then tapped in *W-0000-SH*, pressed the hash key and chose *OPTION 6*.

Five minutes later, Johnny Catbiscuit and Felix Pawson knew exactly what kind of fiendish and odious beings were on the loose. The Realms of Normality needed their help!

CHAPTER ONE
WINTER DRAWERS ON

Earlier that day . . .

'I'm really sorry, Mrs Otterwell,' said Wayne Bunn. 'We had fifty Doggy-Togs delivered yesterday. But they've all gone!'

'Oh dear!' sighed Mrs Otterwell. 'Whatever am I going to do? I've just got to have warm coats for my pets. Or this weather will be the death of them!'

Wayne brushed a frozen dewdrop from the tip of his nose, then said, 'It is cold, isn't it? Let

me check if more are coming in.'

He took off his gloves and tapped the keyboard. Now it was his turn to sigh. 'Suffering snowflakes!' he groaned. 'The computer screen's frozen!'

'Switch it off, then on again,' said Mrs Otterwell. 'That usually works.'

'No, not that sort of frozen!' said Wayne, his breath billowing in the bitter air. 'It's frozen as in . . . *frozen* frozen! Look, it's covered in ice!'

Mrs Otterwell looked at the iced-up computer screen, then she shuddered, saying, 'It is very, *very* cold in here. I'm absolutely perished. And I'm wearing three pairs of my

6

most enormous woolly drawers.'

'Me too!' shivered Wayne. Then he went bright red and said, 'No, I don't mean I'm wearing three pairs of your most enormous woolly drawers, Mrs Otterwell. I just mean I'm absolutely perished, too!' Then he coughed and added, 'Things seem to be going from bad to worse, don't they?'

It was a bitterly cold February morning and, just as he always did on Saturdays, Wayne Bunn was doing what he liked best – helping out at Nicetown pet shop. Because Wayne was absolutely mad about animals!

And he was now having to tell yet another

disappointed customer that they'd completely sold out of Doggy-Togs, Cosy-Cats, Kitty-Mitts and Snug-as-a-Bug Rabbit Rugs! For days, people had been rushing to buy warm coats, bootees and woolly hats for their freezing pets. Even for their hairy guinea pigs and Persian pussy cats. It was *that* cold!

In all his twelve years, Wayne had never

known weather like it. It had been snowing steadily since the middle of February and, as the drifts piled up, the temperatures plummeted. Not only had the pet shop run out of doggy coats, but almost all of the pet food had gone, too. And there was no telling when more would arrive. Customers were being rationed to four tins a week. Quite soon, it would all be gone!

'Then what will happen?' thought Wayne, as he handed Mrs Otterwell her Wuff-Stuff and Miaow-Wow. 'People aren't going to be able to give their own food to their pets. The supermarkets are rationing that, too.'

That evening, Wayne trudged home through

the snowbound streets of Nicetown to the little house where he'd lived with his gran ever since he'd become an orphan.

'More like *Ice*town!' he thought, as he passed gloomy, candlelit houses, each one bristling with clusters of giant icicles. Glancing through open curtains, he saw shivering families and their pets huddled around camping stoves, staring sadly at blank television screens and stone-cold radiators. Others scavenged in their gardens for a few sticks to burn to stay warm until the central heating came back on.

Then, as Wayne crossed the park, he came across a tragic and heartbreaking scene! A tiny

sausage dog was valiantly struggling through the snow, carrying a stick twice its size. As Wayne watched, the gallant little animal made its way towards a small girl who was busy gathering firewood. But then, just as it reached her, it collapsed and lay twitching at her feet, overcome by the cold and worn out. The little girl gave a cry. Dropping her bundle of firewood, she gathered the stricken creature in her arms. Then, before Wayne could help, she rushed off across the park, hugging her beloved pet and sobbing uncontrollably.

As Wayne watched this pitiful little drama, something hit him like a bolt from the blue. He

suddenly knew, without a shadow of a doubt, that this was no ordinary cold snap. This was something different. Very different! Something far more sinister and terrible! Something so sinister and terrible that it could only be the work of that evil genius and mischief-maker, Dr Septacemius J. Septic. The same Dr Septacemius J. Septic who, for as long as Wayne could remember, had been doing his utmost to take over the Realms of Normality, the land where Wayne had lived all his life, and which he loved with all his heart. In his never-ending quest to enslave the good and decent inhabitants of the Realms, Dr Septic was

obsessed with devising ever more evil and cunning plans.

Yes! Wayne knew, without a doubt, that this just had to be yet another of his wicked schemes! For a man of Dr Septic's genius, technical know-how and vast wealth, disastrously disrupting the world's weather patterns would be a piece of cake!

In that astonishing moment, Wayne knew that a great drama was about to unfold. And he also knew that he would soon be playing a crucial part in this drama. Not as Wayne Bunn. But as his other self – the fearless superhero **JOHNNY CATBISCUIT**!

CHAPTER TWO
JOHNNY CATBISCUIT

As soon as Wayne opened his gran's front door, his beloved pets Mr Parks his spaniel, Miss Purrfect his kitten, and Warren his rabbit pounced on him, all desperate for his attention. But Wayne had other things on his mind. So, after giving them the briefest of hugs, he hurried upstairs, accompanied by the latest addition to his menagerie: Felix Pawson, a strikingly handsome tom cat, whom he'd befriended in

the most extraordinary circumstances. In fact, Felix had turned out to be rather more than a friend. And had also proved to possess some *very* remarkable talents!

'Things have gone beyond what you'd call normal, FP!' said Wayne, the moment they were in his bedroom. 'It's time for action! All the other superheroes will already be doing their stuff!'

'You're right!' said Felix. 'There'll be hundreds out there who need our help.'

'Pets and their families cut off by giant snow-drifts!' said Wayne.

'Starving animals in the fields and forests,'

said Felix, looking sad.

'So what are we waiting for?' said Wayne, quickly taking off his glasses. 'Let's go stir some snowflakes!'

He reached into a very ordinary-looking black bin liner and pulled out a magnificent silver vest, with the initials 'JC' on it. This was followed by a golden cape, golden gloves and a pair of gleaming, winged boots. Next came an awesome silver mask. And finally, a sleek and shiny, biometric, plasma-chuffed wrist-pod.

Wayne had the outfit on in seconds. Then, hands on hips, he thrust out his chest, took a deep breath, and said:

'Creatures are freezing and conditions aren't easing
So they need help from Johnny C.
Whatever their plight, he'll see them all right
With help from his sidekick, FP!'

As he did so, an amazing transformation overcame him. First, his entire body began to make a low, hissing, crackling noise. This was accompanied by an unearthly green light, which flickered and danced about him, flashing and pulsating, whilst occasionally mutating into shades of blue and orange. Then, as the hissing died away and the light faded, his entire body began to pulse and heave and ripple.

Muscles throbbed and bulged, sinews stiffened, and flesh grew hard as rock. Now he had the strength of fifty men.

Next, his senses became a thousand times sharper: his hearing so acute that he could hear snow-muffled footsteps five streets away; his vision so powerful that he could zoom in on the details of an object two miles away, even in the dark!

The transformation was complete. Gone were the scrawny shoulders and pale skin of schoolboy Wayne Bunn. Gone too were his puny chest, skinny legs and sticky-out ears. No longer did he look like you could have knocked

him down with a feather. Now it would have taken a ten-ton truck. But even one of those would have come off worse.

Standing in front of Felix, silver vest stretched tight across his broad, muscular chest, was a tall, tanned and extraordinarily good-looking young man. He grinned at felix and gave him the 'thumbs-up', his piercing green eyes sparkling with courage, intelligence and self-assurance.

'You're looking good, Johnny!' said Felix.

'I'm *feeling* good!' replied Johnny Catbiscuit.

'OK!' said Felix. 'My turn!'

Johnny took a smaller version of his own

outfit from the bin liner and placed it in front
of Felix, who now began his amazing tranform-
ation. First, his sinewy, feline form expanded to

twice its normal size. Quite soon, he looked more like a full-grown lynx, rather than a cuddly house cat. Next, his limbs began to stretch and bulge and, as they did, he rose on to his hind legs, now standing almost a metre tall. And finally, his forepaws went through an astonishing change – from small, furry pads into muscular, capable-looking hands, complete with thumbs and fingers, but still with curved and lethal claws. Seizing his dazzling superhero outfit, he had it on in a flash.

Then, with a devil-may-care grin spreading from ear to ear, Felix placed his newly-formed hands on his hips and said, 'Ready to roll!'

'Let's save some souls!' said Johnny.

Dear Gran
have taken the cat out
Might be a little while
Love Wayne XX

CHAPTER THREE
FLYING FURBALLS!

Thirty minutes later, the owner of a riding school was desperately trying to dig her way through giant snowdrifts in an attempt to reach her starving horses. Hearing a noise, she looked up, then let out a cry of astonishment. Streaking across the night sky was a human figure. The woman rubbed her eyes in disbelief. The figure was travelling faster than a jet plane! Beneath it dangled a bulging cargo net.

24

The woman now saw that the flying figure was headed for the stable block where her horses shivered, imprisoned by the snow. The figure swooped effortlessly towards the stables, then began to hover thirty metres above the building.

'How'm I doing?' said Johnny Catbiscuit, as he manoeuvred into position.

'Just fine, superboy!' said Felix Pawson, from the warmth of Johnny's backpack. 'But tell me. Isn't that giant shopping basket even the teensiest bit heavy?'

'Light as a feather!' joked Johnny. 'You're the one who weighs a ton, fatso!'

But it was the huge load that weighed at least

25

a ton. Emergency service workers had packed it for Johnny. It was full to bursting with sacks of oats and barley, cases of animal medicine, dozens of horse blankets, bundles of logs, tins of cat and dog food, flasks of hot tea, bales of straw and hay and much, much more.

'A few metres lower and I'll guide you in,' said Felix. 'I hope this wind doesn't get worse!'

As he spoke, a huge gust caught the net and set it swaying like a massive pendulum, causing Johnny and Felix to lurch terrifyingly.

'It's going to be tricky stabilising this thing,' muttered Johnny.

'*And* you've got to do it twice!' said Felix.

26

'How do you mean?' said Johnny, finally bringing his load under control.

'Well, first you have to stabilise it! Then, you have to *stable*-ise it!'

'Ha! I get you!' laughed Johnny. 'You really are one smart pussy cat!'

The friends' laughter was interrupted by frantic neighing.

'Listen!' said Johnny. 'They're telling me they knew I'd come!'

'Just sounds like neighing to me,' said Felix.

'It wouldn't if you spoke "horse",' said Johnny. 'I'll teach you some day! You picked up "human" quickly enough.'

Then he yelled, 'Hang on down there! Everything's going to be fine!'

'Did you hear that, Angel?' one of the mares said to her shivering foal. 'Johnny Catbiscuit's here. In a few minutes we'll be saved!'

'OK!' said Felix. 'I'll drop down and guide you in.'

With a cry of '*GERONIMO!*', he launched himself into space, plummeting to the ground like a small, furry skydiver.

Minutes later, the load was down. Seizing shovels, Johnny and Felix exploded into action. They'd soon cleared a passage through the drifts and were carrying warm bran mash

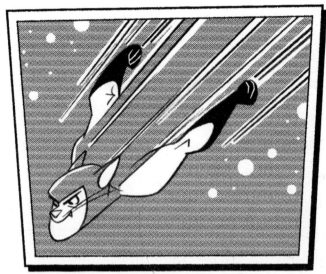

and bedding to the grateful horses.

'You've saved our lives, Johnny Catbiscuit!' snickered a grey mare called Grace. 'How can we ever repay you?'

'There's no need,' said Johnny, patting her neck. 'We're just doing our job!'

29

In the hours that followed, Johnny Catbiscuit and Felix Pawson saved the lives of hundreds of animals and people. Then, just when it looked like their task was almost over, the two chums came across something which left them appalled and dumbfounded. Something so awesome and horrifying that they knew it would stretch their superpowers to their very limits!

It happened when they arrived at a lonely cottage in the beautiful Wotscold hills. Towards the end of their hectic night of non-stop search-and-rescue missions, they'd received an urgent request for assistance. A wildlife film-maker was in need of their help. Having gone

out to pick up supplies, she'd crashed her Earth Rover and was in hospital. So her eight-year-old son and his pet puppy were all on their own at home. His mother was frantic with worry.

'What are we waiting for?' said Johnny. 'Good people need us!'

So Johnny Catbiscuit and Felix Pawson set out on what they thought would be their final mission of the night. How wrong they were!

Soaring over the Wotscolds, Johnny soon spotted the word '**HELP**!' marked out with brightly coloured clothing on a snowy hillside.

'That's our boy, FP!' he cried. 'Let's reunite him and his dog with his mum!'

31

But then they spotted something odd. A trail of destruction had been cut through the woods surrounding the little cottage. Trees had been uprooted and snow and earth churned up.

'That's strange!' said Johnny, zooming in on the cottage with his hyper-vision. 'This is a WAZOCA*!'

Touching down just minutes later, they instantly knew that something was *very* wrong! Everywhere they looked there was chaos. The front door of the cottage lay twenty metres from the house, as if hurled there by some demonic super-force. Windows were smashed and roof tiles scattered around the garden.

*WAZOCA Wildlife Action Zone: Official Conservation Area

32

And splattered everywhere were frozen blobs of disgusting-looking, greenish-yellow goo.

'Hi there!' called Johnny. 'Anyone at home?'

There was no reply. Johnny and Felix raced into the cottage. The havoc inside matched that outside. Furniture smashed, carpets ripped and curtains pulled from their rails. But, most alarming of all, there were huge claw marks everywhere! And there was no sign of the boy or his puppy!

'Maybe he decided to go for help?' said Felix.

'I don't think he'd smash up his own home first!' said Johnny.

'But he's left the house,' said Felix. 'Which

33

means there'll be tracks.'

A minute later they found the tracks. Then Felix let out a long, low hiss. 'Flying furballs!' he gasped. 'Look at those!'

Mixed up with the boy's footprints and his puppy's paw prints were more tracks. They might have been those of a bear. If they hadn't been at least three times bigger!

'Sheesh!' whispered Johnny. 'What made those?'

Then he spotted something in the snow. It was a camcorder. He picked it up, saying, 'FP, I truly hope my hunch is wrong. But I've got a horrible feeling this may hold the key to this

whole mystery!'

He linked the camcorder to his wrist-pod and pressed 'play'.

Just moments after the pals had finished watching the blood-chilling film of that hideous monster's rampage through the cottage, Johnny hit the *OPTIONS* key on his wrist-pod.

35

A young woman's smiling face appeared on the wrist-pod's 3D screen. She was wearing a smart green cap decorated with a badge, bearing the letters '**SSSS**'. 'Hi, Johnny!' she said. 'Thank you for calling Superhero Support Service Solutions. How may I help you?'

'Hi, Jatinder!' said Johnny. 'As you know, we've been dealing with some very extreme weather here in the Realms.'

'I'll say!' said Jatinder. 'Nevertheless, you and your fellow super-beings – **CAPTAIN UNSTOPPABLE**, **Susan the Human Post-It-Note** and **BIODEGRADABLE BOY**, to name but a few – have done great work. Because of your

heroic actions, not a single soul has perished. Good deeds, Johnny!'

'It's what we're here for, Jatinder!' said Johnny. 'But now something else has come up. I'm d-mailing* you an h-peg*. I need some ID on the creature in the film.'

'Not a problem,' said Jatinder. 'I'll have it in a jiffy.'

A moment later, she reappeared, looking very troubled. 'I've run it through our i-db,' she said. 'And I've got some very bad news for you. The creature in the film is an Abominable Snotman!'

*d-mail: dynamic-mail

*h-peg: holo-peg

CHAPTER FOUR
SNOTMEN!

'An Abominable Snotman!' said Johnny. 'What on Space-Speck Earth is one of those?'

'They're part prehistoric polar-ape, part Neanderthal cave-dweller,' continued Jatinder. 'Originally thought to have died out some two thousand years ago. But now the experts aren't so sure. Recent research, based on cave art, ancient Scandiwegian folklore, Viking drinking songs and runic writing suggests that they may

have hung around for a lot longer than that.'

As she spoke, a series of terrifying pictures flashed up on Johnny's wrist-pod multi-screen.

'There was even a report of a couple of them being spotted near a village in Outer Snowberia

in the 1950s. But it wasn't taken seriously. A catastrophe, because a week later, six local children and their pets disappeared, never to be seen again! Snotmen crave the sweeter flesh of children and small animals!'

Felix's fur stood on end, making him look like a small, angry Christmas tree.

'So, what sort of enemy are we dealing with?' said Johnny.

'Take a look at this!' said Jatinder.

A nanosecond later, a file appeared on Johnny's screen.

THE SNOTMAN FILE

HABITAT:

CAVES IN THE SNOWBERIAN ALPS

DIET:

ENTIRELY FLESH EATERS. ONLY SNOTMEN GO OUT TO HUNT WHILE SNOTWOMEN REMAIN AT HOME WEAVING MITTENS, SOCKS AND ENORMOUS PULLOVERS FROM SNOTPERSON FUR DISCARDED DURING THE SPRING MOULT (TO BE WORN LATER, DURING THEIR ONE-HUNDRED-YEAR-LONG 'DORMANCY' PERIODS).

41

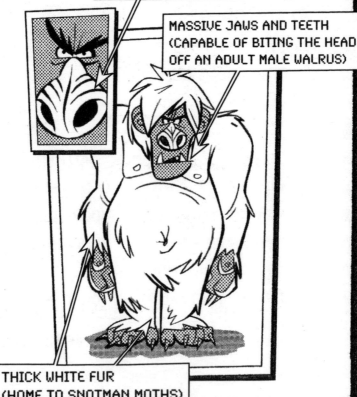

PURPLE AND PINK, SQUISHY, EXPANDABLE NOSE WITH INTERIOR 'SILKY' FUR AND GROOVED NOSTRILS

MASSIVE JAWS AND TEETH (CAPABLE OF BITING THE HEAD OFF AN ADULT MALE WALRUS)

THICK WHITE FUR (HOME TO SNOTMAN MOTHS)

'So, what's with the complicated conk?' said Johnny.

'Well,' said Jatinder, 'in addition to their massive size, terrifying ferocity, lethal claws, awesome strength, phenomenal speed, deafening roar, overpowering body-odour, razor-sharp teeth, poor social skills and terrible bad breath, the Snotmen's most fearsome characteristic is their poisonous, glow-in-the-dark mucus.'

'Yikes, Jatinder!' gasped Felix. 'You're talking . . . TOXIC SNOT!'

'Precisely!' said Jatinder. 'Torrents of the stuff gushes out of their noses when they become excited!'

43

'We're looking at some right now, Jatinder,' said Johnny, surveying the snot-splattered garden.

'It's absolutely lethal!' continued Jatinder. 'When they're really *angry*, the Snotmen sneeze, sending great huge dollops of their hooter-porridge flying in all directions. Whatever it touches, it sticks to it like glue. Once "snotted", the victim experiences terrible wobbliness, followed by a desperate urge to rip off their clothes and leap around, singing "**I've Got a Lovely Bunch of Coconuts!**"!'

'Gross!' said Felix, cautiously sniffing a blob of the frozen snot.

'But that quickly passes,' said Jatinder. 'Next, the "snottee" believes they are a famous figure from history, a wild animal or a piece of fruit. And finally, they simply curl up and fall asleep.'

'Cruel!' said Johnny. 'But do the Snotmen have any weaknesses?'

'Yes,' said Jatinder. 'Poor eyesight and they only know thirty-seven words, including icicle, reindeer, Santa and furball. They're also very slow-witted. For instance, they can only count to one and often mistake their own reflections for rival Snotmen, attacking them without hesitation. And they hate the smell of human happiness.'

'Well, that's all good to know!' said Johnny.

'Yes,' said Jatinder. 'In times gone by, the ancient Scandiwegians sat around their camp-fires telling each other hilarious knock-knock jokes, knowing that their laughter would keep Snotmen at bay.'

'But why has one turned up here?' said Felix.

'Something odd is going on,' said Jatinder. 'Temperatures in the Western Realms are at record lows. But those in Snowberia have risen slightly. Which has resulted in the cryonic unfreezing of the Abominable Snotmen!'

Johnny and Felix exchanged grim looks.

'But none of this could possibly be happening

46

without the schemings of a super-scientist!' continued Jatinder. 'A super-scientist whose genius is only matched by their warped and wicked mind. The sort of maniac who would think nothing of interfering with the delicate balance of the Space-Speck Earth's climate. Just to satisfy their own twisted ends!'

'The evil Dr Septic!' muttered Johnny.

'I'd stake my lives on it!' said Felix.

'It's a no-brainer!' said Jatinder. 'With the aid of electro-magnetic cyclotron exciters, an evildoer of Dr Septic's genius would have no problem disrupting the world's weather.'

'My thoughts exactly!' said Johnny.

47

'But, Johnny!' continued Jatinder. 'There isn't just one Abominable Snotman! There are dozens! Possibly hundreds! We've received a report from the Scandiwegian superhero Harald Hardbones saying that an enormous hunting pack of Abominable Snotmen has rampaged across the Northern Semisphere and crossed the frozen Straits of Despair!'

'Which means they're now in the Realms of Normality!' said Johnny.

'Exactly! But we don't know where! We suspect they'll be heading for a place with lots of people. Somewhere like Wormingham, Drabchester or Nothingham-on-Torrent. Or

48

possibly even Londonland itself! Because that's where they'll find the largest number of fresh victims. And of course, having been deep frozen for so long, they're going to be *very, very* hungry!'

'But what about the one in the film?' said Johnny.

'Abominable Snotmen are always led by a powerful dominant male known as the Snotmaster,' said Jatinder. 'The rest must regularly make it offerings of newly caught prey. This one will have broken away from the main group to find just such an offering.'

'In other words,' sighed Johnny, 'that poor

little boy and his pet puppy!'

'Don't despair!' said Jatinder. 'The offerings must always be presented unharmed. So the boy and his pet will be fine. However, once they're handed over to the Snotmaster . . . ' Jatinder's voice trailed off and her eyes became moist.

'In that case, we must fly!' cried Johnny. 'The sooner we get after that hairy lunkhead, the better! Thanks, Jatinder. You may have just saved the lives of a little boy and his dog!'

'Just doing my job, Johnny!' said Jatinder. 'And thank you for calling Superhero Support Services Solutions. Have a super day!'

CHAPTER FIVE
WHITEMARE!

'If only we'd arrived earlier!' groaned Johnny. 'I could ZAP myself!'

'No!' purred Felix. 'With you out of action, those Abominable Snotmen will have their pick of every pet and child in the land!'

'You're right, sidekick,' said Johnny. 'I can always rely on you to see sense.'

'Well, in cat years, I am older than you!' Felix purred smugly. 'Experience does count

for something!'

'You're right,' said Johnny. 'But I bet you didn't see *this* coming!' Quick as a flash, he flipped Felix into the backpack, then shot skywards, yelling, 'OK, partner! Let's go and zap those sleazeball Snotmen!'

Ten minutes later, as dawn broke, they spotted their quarry.

Head down, jogging along, the shaggy white monstrosity was lumbering through the trees. Tucked under its arms were what looked like bundles of old clothes. But when Johnny zoomed in with his hyper-vision he saw that it was the boy and his puppy!

'Thank goodness,' he yelled. 'Jatinder was right! They seem to be unharmed!'

'Warm too, I'd guess,' added Felix. 'Well, what are we waiting for? Let's hammer that big hairy hardcase!'

'Hang on, sidekick!' said Johnny. 'For the time being, the boy and his pet are safe. And it's absolutely crucial that we find that main group of Snotmen!'

'So we let this one lead us to them!' cried Felix.

'Exactly! Then we rescue the boy and his puppy. After that, we sort out the main mob!'

To begin with, everything went smoothly.

54

Staying just behind the lumbering creature, Johnny cruised at a hundred metres, hyper-scanning the horizon for its companions.

The only thing which gave him cause for concern were the furious snow squalls which were coming with increasing regularity. He was soon covered in a thick layer of freezing snow.

'You look like a flying snowman!' laughed Felix.

'It's all right for y-y-you!' shivered Johnny. 'Tucked up in your little hidey-hole! I'm freeeeeezing!'

But he didn't tell Felix that the rapidly dropping temperatures were making his muscles

numb. Or that he was now having to make *super*, superhuman efforts, just to stay in the air! Or that the worsening weather conditions were making it really hard for him to follow their foe.

However, just when it looked like they might lose sight of the Abominable Snotman completely, Johnny let out a whoop. 'There they are!' he yelled. 'That's just got to be the main mob!'

Squinting hard, Felix saw a long line of shaggy, white figures jogging along a ridge. About a hundred metres ahead of them, a small, dark object, probably a snowmobile, was also moving

across the snow.

'Most likely a farmer getting out of their way!' said Johnny. 'But I don't think he's in any danger. Those Snotmen have got more important things on their minds!'

'They do seem to be in a *very* big hurry!' said Felix. 'Wherever can they be headed for?'

In the next moment, Johnny spotted a mass of distant buildings. 'It's Londonland, FP!' he cried. 'The Abominable Snotmen are making for the Metropolopolis itself!'

'STROMBOLI AND RAVIOLI!' yelled Felix. 'That means thousands and thousands of Londonlanders are going to be completely at

their mercy! And we've no way of warning them. The local authority FARTS* will be clueless!'

'They couldn't do much, even if we did!' cried Johnny. 'Londonland's defence and transport systems are frozen.'

The lone Snotman had also spotted its pals. It was galumphing towards them at an astonishing lick.

'Time to frustrate the furry freaks!' yelled Johnny. 'First we save the boy. Then we hit the hairy hiking hearth-rugs! We're slightly outnumbered, so it isn't going to be a pushover. But we'll certainly give them an experience they'll never remember! We've just got to stop

*FARTS: Fast Action Response Task Squad

58

them reaching Londonland!'

'Way to go, superboy!' purred Felix. 'We'll wallop those whiskery weirdos!'

'They won't know what's hit 'em!' yelled Johnny. 'Let battle commence!'

But then, events took a turn for the worse. All at once, Johnny couldn't tell the difference between the sky and the earth. They were suddenly caught in the wintery hell known as a whiteout! All thoughts of saving the boy and preventing the bewhiskered bogeymen from reaching the Metropolopolis fled from their minds. Now their *own* survival was at stake!

'**NIGHTMARE!**' yelled Felix.

59

'No, FP!' cried Johnny. '**WHITEMARE**!'

Hardly had these words left his mouth, when the atrocious weather brought about their downfall. Despite his super, superhuman efforts, Johnny's already numb and aching muscles now seized up completely. The two pals were suddenly plummeting earthwards, completely unable to help themselves!

Felix clung on for dear life. But such was the velocity and violence of their descent that he was hurled out of the backpack. He prepared for the worst! He knew his landing would be difficult even for a cat of his agility. As he approached the ground, he heard a thud,

60

followed by a groan. But he didn't get a chance
to give it another thought. A second later he
also came down. Then everything went dark.

When Felix came to, the blizzard had passed
and the sun was shining for the first time in

61

weeks. He dragged himself to his feet and shook the snow from his fur. His surroundings felt familiar but he couldn't quite put his paw on where he was. He peered around, hoping to spot his best pal. But there was no sign of Johnny. However, he did see something which made his fur stand on end.

Spread-eagled in the snow next to a stone barn was the Abominable Snotman which had taken the boy. It lay motionless, its mouth open and its eyeballs rolled back in their sockets. Felix was puzzled for a moment. Then he remembered the thud he'd heard. In its mad dash to join its pals, the creature had failed to

see the barn in the whiteout. It had charged straight into it, knocking itself senseless.

But where was the boy and his puppy? Felix's heart sank as all the terrible things which might have happened to them raced through his head. Then he noticed a movement near the Snotman's arm, and a pair of hands emerged from its tangled fur. They were followed by a smiling face. Seconds later, a puppy wriggled out from beneath the Snotman. It bounded over to Felix, wagging its tail furiously.

Johnny wasn't nearly so lucky as Felix. Just seconds after his sidekick had tumbled out of

the backpack, his own heart-stopping descent was halted by a powerful gust of wind. It picked him up as it would a sparrow and hurled him hundreds of metres across the sky. Then Johnny was dropping like a stone, his muscles so petrified with cold that he might have been made of marble. He hit the ground with a bone-rending *crunch* and lost consciousness.

When he opened his eyes, it was to see a circle of fiendish faces staring down at him. It was the Abominable Snotmen! He'd landed right in the middle of them. He was entirely at their mercy!

Johnny took a deep breath and prepared

himself for a thorough 'snotting'. But, instead of blasting him with bogeys, the Snotmen simply stood around him, making sympathetic whimpering noises. Then, even more oddly, the biggest one, obviously the Snotmaster, reached down and helped him to his feet. Then it hit him! Not the Snotmaster, but the realisation that the Abominable Snotmen thought he was one of *them*! His thick coating of snow, combined with their dim eyesight, and even dimmer brains, meant they believed he was a smaller version of themselves.

The Snotmen's hot, stinky breath now began to revive Johnny and he quickly became

super-alert, his brain operating at speeds which would have left a megaputer standing. It was time to turn the situation to his advantage!

The Abominable Snotmen were stamping their feet and rubbing their paws anxiously, whilst making odd groaning noises. Johnny was fluent in hundreds of languages, including Polish, Polar Bear, Prussian, Pilchard, Penguin, Albatross and Arctic Fox, but this was new to him. Nevertheless, he was still able to understand that the Snotmen were troubled and confused. Even the Snotmaster was shaking its head. Then he caught on. They'd lost their way in the whiteout!

He seized his chance. The temperature had risen slightly and feeling was returning to his numbed limbs. It was time for some showing off! With a flick of his heels, Johnny shot into the air thirty metres above the Snotmen's heads. Then, despite the pins and needles fizzing through his muscles, he performed a spectacular loop-the-loop, followed by a perfect figure of eight and a barrel roll!

Heads tipped back, eyes wide, the astounded Snotmen watched his awesome aerobatics in open-mouthed amazement. Then, as he touched down, they began jumping up and down and batting their paws with excitement.

They were ecstatic! One of them could fly!

Now it was Johnny's turn to be astonished. The Snotmen all turned their backs and began wobbling their enormous bottoms at him. At first Johnny was puzzled. But then he realised this must be their way of saying, 'You really are one astonishing Abominable Snotman! We

respect and love you!' (or something like that).
So he wobbled his bottom back at them! And
the Snotmen wobbled their bottoms back
at him. Then Johnny wobbled his bottom back
at them. And the Snotmen wobbled theirs back
at him!

Of course, the bottom-wobbling session
could have gone on all day. But Johnny decided
it was time to take control. He began jogging
on the spot. The Snotmen copied him. Still
spot-jogging, he pointed to a distant, unseen
destination (making sure it was in the opposite
direction to Londonland). The Snotmen did
likewise, eagerly looking to Johnny for further

instructions. They were his! They would follow him to the ends of the Earth. All he had to do now was to lead them away from Londonland!

So, shouting something which he hoped sounded like, 'Forward, my bewhiskered brothers!' (but in Snotman), Johnny rushed off, with a couple of hundred extremely excited Abominable Snotmen all charging after him.

He wasn't sure where he was taking them. He supposed he could run in endless circles, until the Snotmen eventually collapsed, exhausted. Or he could lead them into a really big maze where they'd be lost forever. However, he didn't know where a really big maze was.

But he did know one thing. He had to keep the Snotmen well away from their quarry – the pets, children and citizens of Londonland.

Quarry! The idea struck him in a flash. He and Felix had flown over a really deep one just before the weather had closed in. It couldn't be more than a few miles away.

Five minutes later, Johnny and his new 'friends' were thundering towards the point where the distance across the cliffs of the quarry was narrow enough for an Abominable Snotman to leap all the way across. Well, almost narrow enough!

CHAPTER SIX
THE QUARRY

Johnny cleared the chasm effortlessly. Roaring with excitement, fifty ecstatic Abominable Snotmen followed him, enthusiastically hurling themselves into space, one hundred per cent confident they'd reach the other side.

The look of surprise on their faces when they realised they weren't quite going to make it was a picture. At first, the hairy half-wits attempted to run the last few metres! But this

only made them look extremely silly. Then, realising the 'running' wasn't working, some of them actually tried to 'swim' to the other side. Which made them look even sillier. And finally, a couple of the more adventurous ones made a rather half-hearted attempt at 'flying'. Which was just hilarious! Less than a nanosecond later, they began plummeting towards the

quarry bottom, windmilling their arms and bellowing in dismay. A mixture of splats, thuds and angry grunts followed.

Johnny rejoined the Snotmen still running towards the quarry, urging them on with shouts and gestures. With victory so near, he didn't

want them to lose their enthusiasm for 'cordless bunjee jumping', as he now thought of it.

But then his hopes of wiping out those hairy half-wits vanished like a snowflake in a sauna. All at once, the Snotmen stopped hurling themselves into space. Every single one of them was now staring at Johnny in a manner which could only be described as 'extremely unfriendly'.

For a moment, Johnny was at a loss as to why. But then he heard an ominous 'splish'. It was followed by an even more ominous 'splosh'. It didn't take a genius to work out what was happening. But he thought he'd take a look anyway. When he did, his suspicions were

confirmed. A small avalanche of ice and snow was sliding from his body. Yes, his Snotman 'fur' was disintegrating, melted by his body heat! He was exposed, in all his superhero glory!

'Ah well!' mused Johnny. 'Even superheroes can't think of everything!'

Quite understandably, the Abominable Snotmen weren't too happy that they'd been so cruelly tricked. And they were absolutely furious that so many of their friends were at the bottom of the quarry. So they showed their displeasure in a way that only an Abominable Snotman can. Like a horrid vegetable stew, huge globbets of greenish-yellow gunk began to

ooze and bubble from their noses. Then they rushed at Johnny.

But, just as he was preparing to take on a hundred or so extremely annoyed Abominable

Snotmen, Johnny was knocked to the ground by a massive blow to the back of his head. Seconds later, he opened his eyes to see a familiar face staring down at him. A face which, despite its snow goggles and furry hat, Johnny recognised as the one belonging to the evil Dr Septic.

The evil Dr Septic who had, just moments earlier, silently slid on to the scene astride his shiny-black skidoo. Yes, the very same skidoo which Johnny and Felix had seen the Snotmen following across that snowy ridge just half an hour earlier (so much for fleeing farmers!).

'Mr Catflap,' he rasped, in a voice which

made Johnny think of rusty razor blades being crushed in a food processor. 'With the help of these bearded boneheads,' here he nodded towards the Snotmen, who were now bottom-waggling at Dr Septic as though their lives depended on it, 'I am about to descend upon Londonland and create a spectacle of such horror that even the Emperors of Ancient Rome would be jealous. And you almost spoiled it! A thousand ways of making you the most miserable super-mortal on Space-Speck Earth are rushing into my head. But I'm already late for my "event"! So they will have to wait. For the time being, I'm going to . . . "put you on ice"!'

80

Turning to the Snotmen, Dr Septic began slowly wagging his forefinger from side to side, whilst raising and lowering his eyebrows. The Snotmen instantly focused their entire attention on his moving finger and his wiggling

eyebrows, utterly mesmerised by them.

'Suffering sandpipers!' thought Johnny. 'He's got them hypnotised!'

Dr Septic clapped his hands and four of the Snotmen seized Johnny and carried him to a part of the quarry where its fifty-metre walls fell away to a vast, frozen lake.

'I will return, Mr Dogbiscuit!' growled Dr Septic. 'Then I will defrost you. After which, I will . . . go to work on you!'

As the Snotmen started swinging Johnny backwards and forwards, Dr Septic began to chant, 'With a ONE . . . and a TWO . . . and a . . .'

But Dr Septic had forgotten that Snotmen can only count to one. So, by the time he reached '. . . JOLLY GOOD THREE!', Johnny had already hit the ice.

Not only that, but the Snotmen had also got very carried away with their swinging. So, instead of landing at the lake edge, where the ice was at its thickest (as Dr Septic had intended), Johnny landed in the very middle. And because the ice was thinner here, he crashed through the frozen surface and disappeared!

'You Neanderthal numbskulls!' raged Dr Septic, shaking his fist at the bewildered Snotmen. 'You Palaeolithic pinheads! You've

blinking well sunk him!'

But then he calmed down, shrugged and sighed, 'No matter! At least it'll be one less interfering superhero to worry about. And anyway, we have more important things to do!'

Then, leaping aboard his supercharged skidoo, he once more began finger-wagging and eyebrow-jiggling, as he yelled, 'To Londonland, my snotty simpletons! Your din-dins await!'

And he sped off, followed by his Snotmen, just as the ice was re-forming over Johnny.

CHAPTER SEVEN
LONDONLAND

Of course, Johnny didn't die in the flooded quarry. Mere mortals wouldn't have lasted a microsecond. But Johnny, being made of superbly superior stuff, survived. Instead of killing him, the freezing water actually woke him up. So much so that, a few minutes later, he burst back through the ice.

But he was still extremely wet and, as everyone knows, if you stay wet, you get a lot

colder! This applies to superheroes, too. So, having been a Snotman, Johnny now became an Iceman. In fact, he soon became so crisply cocooned in a thick coat of crunchy, crackly ice that movement became almost impossible. Which prevented him from flying out of the

quarry. Or scaling its massive walls!

He was well and truly trapped! And getting colder by the second. Realising that the most likely outcome of his predicament was going to be of the 'Unhappily Ever After' variety, Johnny began to skate around the lake, in an effort to warm up. Not easy, when you've just become completely 'double-glazed'. But Johnny did his best, humming those waltz tunes which proper ice skaters whirl 'n' twirl to, and all the time trying to think of warm things, like blazing log fires and affectionate pets. Affectionate pets like . . . Felix Pawson! Oh no! What had become of Felix? Suddenly gripped with anxiety

for his friend's well-being, Johnny crossed his fingers and prayed that he was OK.

But then, as if in answer to his prayers, a voice yelled, 'I don't believe it! The entire population of the Metropolopolis is about to be set upon by hundreds of gigantic flesh-eating furry fiends and you decide to go ice-skating! Call yourself a superhero? You ought to be ashamed of yourself!'

And Johnny looked up just in time to see Felix doing his furry skydiver impression down into the quarry.

'What kept you?' groaned Johnny, as Felix secured a lifting harness to Johnny and gave

the 'paws-up' to the horses at the quarry edge. 'And are the boy and his dog OK?'

'They're both back with his mum,' said Felix. 'That's definitely a job well done, partner!'

With Grace the mare taking the lead, the horses pulled, and Johnny was hauled to the top of the quarry, where the lady from the riding stables wrapped him in warm blankets.

Then Felix told him about landing next to the unconscious Snotman at the very spot where they'd begun their night's adventures, and how he and the stables lady had followed the Snotmen tracks and found Johnny in the quarry. 'You looked like an Iceman!' said Felix.

'I am a "nice" man!' joked Johnny.

Then he remembered that Dr Septic and the Abominable Snotmen were probably rampaging around Londonland, causing untold harm and misery while he made corny jokes, so he leapt to his feet and said, 'Ready to roll, FP!'

Five minutes later, Johnny Catbiscuit and his heroic little sidekick were zooming over the picturesque villages of Outer Londonland faster than they'd ever flown before. Then, as Johnny went hypersonic and Felix felt the G-forces give him the fur-do he'd never wanted, they streaked towards the heart of the Metropolopolis.

One glance at the snowy streets told them that Dr Septic and his HUMONGOUS HAIRBALLS had arrived. The evidence of their terrible rampage was everywhere: shop windows smashed, broken furniture littering the icy pavements, cars upended and shopping scattered everywhere, as panic-stricken

91

Londonlanders fled from the hairy menaces.

And what of those Londonlanders? How had they fared as these terrors from the wintry wastelands of Snowberia came galumphing into their beloved city, without so much as a 'do you mind'? Well, as far as Johnny and Felix were able to make out, thousands of them had already taken refuge in the great honeycomb of tunnels which was underground Londonland.

But then, as they soared over the swanky Best End, it became clear that not everyone had managed to reach these havens of safety! They now began to see scattered groups of people slipping and sliding along the snowy

pavements, comforting their sobbing children and howling pets as they cast anxious glances over their shoulders, terrified that they might become victims of these monsters from they-knew-not-where!

Then, as one crowd of terrified Londonlanders raced past another going in the opposite direction, a boy shouted, 'They're behind us. Run for your lives!'

Only to have a girl in the other crowd yell, 'No, they're not! They're behind *us*! Run for *your* lives!'

And with that, each group immediately turned and ran off in the direction from which

they'd just come.

'I'm getting conflicting intelligence here!' cried Johnny, still unseen by the panic-stricken crowds, as he used his hyper-hearing to tune in on their shouts and screams. 'It's time we got the bigger picture!'

They shot up another fifty metres. Now, all the magnificent sights of snow-covered Londonland were spread out below them: the Houses of Parsleymint, Duckingham Palace, St Pauline's Cathedral, and many more.

Normally, the chums would have relished this wonderful sight. But what they saw only made them gasp in dismay, as the full extent of

the horror, panic and chaos which gripped the icebound city became clear. Not just dozens, but hundreds of unlucky souls were still out on the freezing streets. And, like giant sheepdogs, Dr Septic's Abominable Snotmen were herding every single one of them towards the capital's most central point . . . Superhero Square itself!

And it was there, under the stony gaze of all those great and good superheroes from the past: Palaeolithic Lad, Codpiece Carlisle, Cardigan Bootstop, Erasmus the Human Bicycle and Crinoline Martha, to name but a few, that the Abominable Snotmen launched their assault on the good folk of Londonland.

CHAPTER EIGHT
SUPERHERO SQUARE

Fifteen minutes later, on one side of the square, one hundred and fifty Abominable Snotmen grunted and snorted as the Snotmaster paced backwards and forwards. It paused only to scratch its frighteningly greasy armpits or to sniff its huge and smelly bottom. And, on the other side, stood just fifty very brave and very cold policemen. A few had on their uniforms, but most were dressed in shorts, T-shirts and

trainers. They were clutching table-tennis bats and looking very, very unhappy.

The arrival of the Snotmen had taken the policemen by surprise. They'd been having their weekly ping-pong tournament. And, as Inspector Hector Vector of the Metropolopitan Sector said later, 'When you're enjoying a knockabout, the last thing you expect is an invasion of Abominable Snotmen. I dunno . . .

whatever next!'

Nevertheless, the policemen were now ready to make the final sacrifice in the defence of the Realms. They were the only thing that stood between the Snotmen and the huge crowd of children, pets and grown-ups which the shaggy monsters had herded into Superhero Square.

And, to make matters worse, Johnny knew that somewhere among that vast throng there lurked the evil Dr Septic. Using the cover of the crowd, he would be controlling the Snotmen's every move with that sinister 'tick-tocking' finger and those evil bouncing eyebrows.

'**OK, SUPERBOY!**' said Felix, as the dynamic

duo touched down in deserted Cardigan Gardens, just next to Superhero Square. **'LET'S GO ZAP THAT SLEAZEBALL SEPTIC!'**

'No way, FP!' said Johnny, indicating the crowds. 'You haven't a cat in Londonland's chance of finding him. And he's bound to be in disguise. He could be anyone. Like that dread-locked Rastafarian carrying the goldfish!'

'Or the five-year-old with the ginger tabby,' agreed Felix. 'So, boss, what do we do?'

'I've got an idea, FP!' said Johnny. 'But it will mean us working harder and faster than we've ever done before!'

'Sounds cool!' said Felix. 'Tell me about it!'

Seconds later, the plucky pair were putting Johnny's super-plan into action. And, as they began their race against time, so the Abominable Snotmen commenced their attack on the brave police officers of Londonland.

First, the Snotmaster let out an earth-shattering roar, so loud it broke all six thousand windows in the nearby houses of Parsleymint. Then, as the shivering crowds looked on, petrified, the Abominable Snotmen began their 'performance'. Their eardrum-bursting bellows echoing around Superhero Square, they thrust out their chests and put their paws in the air.

'Brilliant!' yelled Felix, pausing briefly from his high-speed 'snow-sculpting' project, which was now demanding every last ounce of his and Johnny's energy. 'They've surrendered!'

'Of course they've not surrendered!' said Johnny. 'Why would they?'

As if to prove him right, the Snotmen now brought down their paws and slapped their massive thighs with a mighty *THWACK!*

'Ouch!' muttered Felix. 'I bet that hurt!'

The Snotmen now began rhythmically slapping their thighs and stamping their feet. **THWACK!** **STAMP!** **STAMP!** *THWACK!* **STAMP!** **STAMP!** they went.

'It's a war dance!' whispered Felix.

Without missing so much as a **THWACK!** or a **STAMP!**, the Snotmen now began the 'face-pulling'. It was so frightening that, at one point, it looked as if the entire Metropolopitan Police Force would run away. But they didn't, apart from one young constable, who was suddenly seized by an urgent need to nip to the loo.

First, the Snotmen made their eyes go so big that they looked as if they'd pop right out and go bouncing across Superhero Square. Next, they stuck out their huge purple tongues, wiggling and lashing them from side to side. Then, paws a-thwacking, feet a-stamping, eyes a-bulging, and tongues a-waggling, the Snotmen

 began to advance on the terrified policemen.

Had our dynamic duo not already been so mind-bogglingly busy being 'creative' in the adjoining Cardigan Gardens, they would have certainly gone to the policemen's aid. But Johnny and Felix had pets and children to think of (not to mention, several tons of snow to shape!). This time, the cops would just have to take care of themselves!

'I wonder what's going to happen next?' said Felix.

'I think they're going to sneeze,' said Johnny.

'Oh dear!' said Felix.

CHAPTER NINE
SNOTTED!

Johnny was right. And when those Snotmen did finally sneeze, it resembled nothing less than eight hundred absolutely **ENORMOUS EXPLOSIONS** taking place inside one hundred and fifty **GIANT BLUNDERBUSSES**. ATCHOO! ATCHOO! ATCHOO! ATCHOO! ATCHOO! ATCHOO! ATCHOO! ATCHOO! ATCHOO!

The police-
men didn't
stand a chance.
They were slapped by a storm of snot.
Hammered by a hurricane of hooter-goo!
Battered by a broadside of bogeys!

SPLATT! SPLATT! SPLATTTETY SPLATT! SPLATTY SPLATT! SPLATT!

Leaping about, they desperately tried to
dodge the showers of snozzle-slime, slapping

wildly at the flying conk-crud with their table-tennis bats. But they might as well have been trying to make rain return to the clouds.

Inevitably and tragically, the monsoon of mucus began to take its toll. Within seconds, the police officers began wobbling furiously, like blancmanges on a runaway dessert trolley.

Then they began ripping off their clothes. Tunics, T-shirts, shorts, helmets, trousers, boots and police-issue string vests went flying, like a month's worth of washing being blown away in a gale. One gigantic pair of policeman's trousers landed '**PLOP**!' on the head of no less a person than Hector Vector, Head Inspector of

the Metropolopitan Sector. But was he bothered? No, he was too busy ripping off his own uniform.

All at once, at least forty police officers, dressed only in their undies, were leaping around Superhero Square, clapping their hands, grinning like idiots and singing, '**I've Got a Lovely Bunch of Coconuts!**' at the tops of their voices.

Then, as quickly as it had begun, the dancing and singing ended and a very tall policeman yelled, '**I'm a banana from the coast of Gheeana! I'm very appeeeeeling!**'

While another shouted, 'That's as maybe, but I'm a bush baby! And I love bananas!' Then he attempted to bite off the 'banana's' head!

And so began the next round of lunacy, with policemen imitating every sort of fruit and animal imaginable and claiming to be everyone from Bodice Eva, Queen of the Ancient Baritones, to William Shapespeaker!

It wasn't a pretty sight. However, just as Jatinder had said, one by one the clucking, grunting, yelling and neighing policemen began to curl up on the snowy pavements. They were soon off in the Land of Plod, snoring peacefully and dreaming of retirement to Letsby Avenue.

And what had the Snotmen been doing during all this silliness (apart from sneezing, of course). Well, nothing actually. Instead of rushing

forward and tearing the defenceless officers into tiny, tiny pieces, they had simply stood and watched, their faces expressionless and eyes blank. Why? Because Dr Septic was 'saving' them! Hypnotically holding them back for his 'grand finale'! In other words, the attack on all those good and decent souls who cowered and whimpered behind the sleeping policemen.

But now Dr Septic was ready to unleash his furry fiends. Slipping away from the crowd, he gave the signal for his mob of starving flesh-eaters to attack. They rushed at the screaming, howling, yelping children, pets and parents.

CHAPTER TEN
HeadBangers

Which was the exact moment that Johnny put his daring plan into action. Just seconds before the charging Snotmen reached their victims, he leapt on to the broad granite shoulders of the great and noble Cardigan Bootstop himself. After which, he 'thunder-clapped'* so violently that the resultant **BANG!** would surely have shattered all of the windows in the nearby Houses of Parsleymint (had they not already

* Method of hand-clapping unique to superheroes, which usually produces a bang in excess of 120 decibels

been shattered by the Snotmaster).

It got the result he'd intended. The charging Snotmen stopped in their tracks. And the sobbing crowds turned to behold the legendary boy superhero who would soon be saving them from the Snowberian menaces!

Now, in a voice so loud and booming that it did shatter several hundred windows, this time in the neighbouring Ministry of the Dense (Johnny later paid for them to be replaced) he yelled, **'HELLO, EVERYONE! NICE TO BE HERE! A FUNNY THING HAPPENED TO ME ON THE WAY TO THE METROPOLOPOLIS TODAY!'** and he went on to tell them one of the funniest

funny stories* they'd ever heard in their lives! So funny, that in spite of their terrible predicament, they began to howl and howl, not with terror, but with happiness!

But Johnny wasn't finished. Before the crowd could recover from his first humdinger of a joke, he told them another, so screamingly brilliant that the blissful crowds were now almost wetting themselves with laughter.

And, of course, just as Johnny and Felix had planned, the delightful odour of all that human happiness had exactly the opposite effect on the stunned Snotmen. In just seconds, they were groaning with misery and thrusting their

* Told to Johnny by Felix Pawson

112

paws up their noses, in order to stop the hated aroma of human merriment streaming into their squalid little brains.

And, as his Snotmen suffered, Dr Septic seethed, his hypnotic hold on the creatures overwhelmed by this great tide of hilarity. He knew full well that any attempt to interfere would expose him for the evildoer he was. And, even though he still had hopes of a last-minute miracle, he knew that the game was up, and that it was time to be slipping away. And, of course, like any sensible super-villain, he'd

113

already planned his 'exit strategy', secretly parking his skidoo in a nearby street, and even going to the trouble of popping a fistful of coins into the nearest parking meter.

But back to Johnny. With the crowds happy and the Snotmen stunned, it was time for him to put the final phase of his plan into operation. Knowing that even the most dim-witted Snotman would realise he was responsible for the massive wafts of happiness which were 'getting up their noses', Johnny and Felix deliberately placed themselves squarely in front of them and began to taunt them. They yelled, **'COME ON THEN, YOU HAIRY**

HEARTH-RUGS! LET'S SEE WHAT YOU'RE MADE OF!' and pulled the very faces which the Snotmen had pulled in their 'war dance'!

It was the final straw for the Snotmen! Bellowing with rage, they chased the superhero and his sidekick into Cardigan Gardens, intent on tearing them into bite-size super-morsels, the Londonlanders all but forgotten.

But then, as the Abominable Snotmen entered that lovely Londonland square, they

115

skidded to a halt. They were **FLABBERSMACKED!** They couldn't believe their short-sighted eyes! Dotted around the square and its surrounding streets were the magnificent results of Johnny and Felix's furious snow-sculpting project. Or, as it appeared to their pursuers, another huge gang of Abominable Snotmen. What's more, every one of these 'NEW-SNOTMEN-ON-THE-BLOCK' was staring at them in a way which could only be described as challenging!

Well, Snowberian Snotmen simply do not walk away from that sort of thing! They meet it head on! So with a huge, 'IT'S ALL OR NOTHING!' roar, they lowered their heads and charged the infuriatingly cool and cocky new rivals, like a tribe of enraged goats.

The Abominable Snotmen must have been doing at least seventy miles an hour when they crashed into the street signs, statues, bollards, trees, phone booths, bus shelters, traffic lights and other very solid objects, which Johnny and Felix had swiftly and carefully hidden inside the 'rival gang of Snotmen' (or 'snowmen'). And crashing into something like a tree trunk or

signpost at that sort of speed is guaranteed to result in unhappiness. Even if you are an Abominable Snotman whose brain is at least eighty per cent pure gristle.

Some of the Snotmen actually bounced off the 'enemy', while others simply slumped to the ground with looks of disbelief on their big dozy faces. In seconds, there were at least one hundred unconscious Abominable Snotmen sprawled around Cardigan Gardens. The rest staggered around, wondering what had hit them. Then they began fighting amongst themselves, believing each other to be the 'enemy', and delivering such knockout punches that

they quickly joined their pals in the land of 'LIGHTS OUT, NO ONE AT HOME!'

All but the Snotmaster, that is. Possessing a brain slightly superior to those of its thick-witted pals, it had quite rightly worked out that all was not as it seemed. So it decided to give the head-butting a miss. It was also able to grasp (just like Dr Septic) that the game was more or less up. So it hightailed it out of there.

But it wasn't defeated just yet! For a start, it was still very hungry. And also very, very angry. So, rather than heading for the frozen sea and making its way back to Snowberia, it decided to go hunting.

CHAPTER ELEVEN
BLESS YOU!

In a cobbled street in Olden Londonland, a most terrifying scene was being played out. A man and woman were stumbling along the icy pavements, closely followed by a little girl clutching a tiny kitten. Twenty metres behind the little girl, long strands of purple drool dangling from its massive jaws, its eyes glinting with pure evil, came the Snotmaster! It bellowed, snorted and grunted, ecstatic with

the thrill of the chase, as the gap between it and the fleeing child shrank with its every step!

Then, horror of horrors, the little girl slipped, and her kitten tumbled from her grasp. But, instead of doing the sensible thing, and leaving the little creature to make its own escape, she stopped and tried to pick it up. This brave act almost cost her her life!

The Snotmaster was on her in a flash! Moments later it stood before her horrified parents, their screaming child and her kitten gripped in its huge paw. Then it opened its enormous jaws and raised them to its steaming, cavernous mouth, preparing to pop them in.

But that's as far as it got. At that instant, there was a sudden **WHOOOOOSH!**, and something streaked along the street, faster than an intercontinental missile! A microsecond later, Johnny Catbiscuit's iron-hard fist hit the Snotmaster squarely on the chin, with all the

force of a speeding subatomic particle collider!
It let out an enormous yell of surprise and
anger, dropping the little girl and her kitten.
Felix was there in a flash, swiftly shepherding
them back to the waiting arms of her parents.

The Snotmaster now turned the full force of
its fury on Johnny. Roaring with rage and pain,
it rushed at him, frothy green gloop bubbling
from its nostrils, its eyes glowing red for danger.
There was no doubt about it! The creature was
about to sneeze. And Johnny knew that to be
put out of action by a devastating blast of its
toxic snot would be disastrous. Not only for
himself, but for Felix and the little family! So

he took a desperate gamble.

Launching himself at the charging Snotmaster, he performed a dazzling triple somersault, springing right up into the creature's hideous face, arms outstretched. Then, as he hung in mid-air for a picosecond, he rammed his clenched fists right up inside the Snotmaster's warm and gooey nostrils!

WHUMMMMPHHH! Like that!

The look of astonishment on the Snotmaster's big stupid face was something Johnny would treasure for years to come. But then, from somewhere deep within its huge head, there came ominous rumblings, rather

like an approaching tropical storm. Realising something wasn't right, its eyes flashed this way and that. Then, it went berserk, desperately trying to wrench Johnny from its nostrils.

However, despite its frenzied efforts to

dislodge him, Johnny heroically hung in there, straining to strengthen his grip on its snot-box. If he lost it, he was done for. Grasping handfuls of nose hairs in one fist, he thrust his other one even further up its nasal cavity. Then, once *that* fist was well and truly wedged in its narrowest and most distant reaches, he did the same with the first. And only just in time. Because, at this point, the Snotmaster sneezed.

'Bless you!' yelled Felix, diving for cover.

The explosion inside the Snotmaster's head was similar to that of a fifty megaton nuclear device being detonated inside a very small strong box. Johnny felt the shock waves race

down his arms, then reverberate around his entire body. But still he hung there, fists firmly jammed deep inside the creature's nostrils.

It sneezed again.

'Bless you, again!' yelled Felix. 'You really ought to take something for that!'

This second explosion made the first one seem like a damp squib. Such was its power that the Snotmaster's huge, pink-veined eye-balls actually began to revolve in their sockets. Then, much to its own, and everyone else's, surprise, its eyebrows flew off. And finally, as if to add humiliation to injury, torrents of white-hot snot began to gush from its *ears*! It sat

down on the pavement, looking as upset as if it had just discovered it had accidentally put its winning lottery ticket through a shredder.

The Snotmaster was done for. Or, 'ALL SNOTTED OUT!' as Felix later described it. There was no telling what damage that second internal explosion had done to its already-addled brain.

Taking care not to let the smallest drop of the toxic snot fall on his skin, Johnny slowly removed his fists from its nostrils, then stood back to survey his 'handiwork'.

Felix joined him. 'Nice work, boss!' he said. 'You were certainly "up to your elbows" in it!'

But before Johnny had a chance to laugh at

his sidekick's joke, the little girl's father rushed up to him and cried, 'That's the bravest thing I ever did see! You saved my daughter's life. I really must shake you by the hand!'

Then he noticed Johnny's snot-drenched gauntlets and said, 'Hmmm, perhaps some other time.'

'Well, that seems to be that, then!' said Johnny, as he and Felix inspected the shattered Snotmaster. 'Job more or less done!'

'Certainly looks like it, boss,' said Felix. 'Apart from old "you know who"!'

'Who is probably speeding homewards on his turbocharged three hundred kilometres per

hour skidoo. With such a massive head start on us, we'd be wasting our time trying to catch him.'

'Dr Septic will keep until another day,' said Felix. Then he grinned, saying, 'Hey, have you seen where we are?'

'No, where are we?' said Johnny.

Felix pointed to the sign on the wall.

ROYAL BOROUGH OF LONDONLAND

SNOTTING HILL

'That's quite funny!' laughed Felix. 'Is it snot?'

But what of Dr Septic? Did he hang around to see what would happen next? Of course he did! He just couldn't resist the temptation. So he stayed, but only long enough to see his Snowberian simpletons beating themselves brainless on the street furniture of Cardigan Gardens. Realising that the game was most definitely up, he raced back to his skidoo.

Then, vowing to extract the sort of revenge upon Johnny Catbiscuit which would most certainly earn him a much-prized place in the Super-Villains Hall of Shame, Dr Septic began the long journey home.

And, as that evil and justly-thwarted villain

sped through the rapidly-melting snow, his weather-warping scheme abandoned and his plans for the domination of the Realms of Normality once more in tatters, Johnny Catbiscuit and Felix Pawson returned to Nicetown.

Here, as the birds sang and the flowers

blossomed in the warm, spring sunshine, they once more became Wayne Bunn and his pet pussycat and made their way to Wayne's gran's. Hardly had they got through her front door than, without even bothering to ask where they'd been, she began bombarding Wayne with news of all the astonishing events which had been taking place down in Londonland.

So, as his adoring (but somewhat absent-minded) gran told him all about the awesome Johnny Catbiscuit's astonishing defeat of the Abominable Snotmen, all young Wayne could do was listen, wide-eyed with amazement.

And finally, her story almost finished, his

gran said, 'And they're going to take the Snotmen back to Snowberia. So they'll never ever bother us again. And it's all thanks to that amazing young superhero, Johnny Catbiscuit! What *ever* will he do next?'

Then she sighed and said, 'I bet you wish you could be like him, our Wayne!'

'Oh, I do, Gran, I do!' said Wayne, giving Felix the briefest of winks.

THE END

§§§§

Captain Unstoppable

Four times winner of the Superhero of the Year Award, **CAPTAIN UNSTOPPABLE** is descended from a long line of superheroes, including Crinoline Martha and Cardigan Bootstop. Once, he was so determined to prove his devotion to duty that he wandered the streets of Busyville in his super-suit, asking passers-by if they were 'all right', then reminding them that he was 'only too willing to help'. An old couple took him at his word and he cleaned out their pet guinea pigs' hutches, mowed their lawn, did their ironing and pegged out their washing, all in his spangled cape, golden bootees and spandex body stocking. He's never done that again!

SPECIAL POWERS

He has seemingly unlimited superstrength. He once pulled a fully loaded **GIGANTI-JET**™ aeroplane, with its 972 passengers, for two miles along the runway of Drabchester Airport using just a length of cable and his front teeth. Not because the passengers were

in any danger, but simply because he 'felt like it'.

SPECIAL POWERS

Captain Unstoppable was nine when he spotted a couple of bank robbers bundling three terrified hostages into their getaway car. They sped off faster than 200 miles per hour and the young superhero gave chase, still in his school uniform. After a thrilling pursuit involving overturned dustbins, flocks of chickens and men carrying sheets of plate glass, the plucky lad caught up with them on the MVII Superhighway. He seized the rear end of their vehicle, brought it to a halt and rescued the hostages. When questioned by the police about his remarkable turn of speed, young Ken told

137

them that he had been feeling 'energetic'. He was later told off by GOSH[*] for performing a rescue in plain clothes.

ACHILLES HEEL

He has purplebrasproutophobia (for more on this, please read *Johnny Catbiscuit and the Stolen Secrets*). Captain Unstoppable is very fond of puddings and if he doesn't exercise often he puts on weight. He once split his super-suit mid-rescue, and was unable to fly with the two scientists he was rescuing from a ferocious Radium Ogre which had broken out of its tank in their laboratory. He had to race off down the road, the Radium Ogre in hot pursuit, a scientist tucked under each arm, and

a huge tear in his super-suit exposing his extremely flabby and wobbly super-bottom.

OTHER CHARACTERISTICS

Captain Unstoppable is an 'old school superhero', who regards polite behaviour and 'being well turned out' as a priority. So he regularly turns up to rescues wearing a tie and sporting a smart silk handkerchief tucked into the top pocket of his sparkly, electric-blue supersuit. He always bows politely to friend and foe before: a) rescuing them or b) giving them a thrashing.

SIDEKICK

The 14-year-old Dexter Doodlebug. Captain Unstoppable once gave him a telling-off for

turning up to a rescue in a woolly hat and scruffy trainers rather than his silver mask and winged bootees. Dexter is obsessed with 'drama' and believes everything he does should be carried out with superhero flair. He once hurled himself through Captain Unstoppable's windows to announce that something terrible was happening in Downtown Drabchester, rather than ringing his doorbell.

DAY TO DAY IDENTITY

Captain Unstoppable is actually Ken Chapman of Chapman's Chippy, Nicetown, Realms of Normality NV23 6RN. When he's not carrying out death-defying rescues, he can be found

selling haddock and fritters, curried saveloy and mushy peas to the likes of Wayne Bunn. He has never married but has had romances, including one with Moth Woman, which ended disastrously when he took her out for a romantic candle-lit dinner.

PETS

Captain Unstoppable has a whippet called Norman and a tortoise called Flash. Norman likes curried saveloy and, to Captain Unstoppable's annoyance, never gets any bigger, no matter how many he eats. Flash is the strong silent type.

SUPERHERO PROFILE

Susan
the Human-Post-It-Note

Susan (23) first discovered she was 'special' at the age of five when playing hide and seek at a friend's house. Desperately looking for a hiding place, she discovered that she was not only able to make herself go completely flat, but was also able to copy the rose-patterned wallpaper which covered the walls of her friend's living room and to attach herself to it,

so she was invisible to her pals. However, she gave herself away by giggling and snorting uncontrollably, which led to several of her friends having to have therapy with the local child psychologist.

ACHILLES HEEL

Susan is frightened of soup, drawing pins and the word 'nullify'.

SPECIAL POWERS

Susan has tremendous sticking-power and is able to flatten herself – from cardboard-thin to almost-not-there translucent. She is also able to take on the characteristics of an infinite number of materials, including cling-film, postage stamps, packaging, designer labels,

litter and junk mail. Her latest and proudest achievement is copying all three thousand shades from the colour chart of a well-known paint manufacturer.

OTHER SUPERPOWERS

If she is really well rested, has eaten sago pudding, and there happens to be a waning gibbous moon, Susan is able to dissolve herself in any liquid (with the exception of Cola) or dehydrate completely. These occasions are rare. This is understandable, as she was once drunk by Murgatroyd Doom after dissolving herself in his mango smoothie. She doesn't talk about this.

FIRST EVER SUPER-MISSION

The evil Professor Elvis Troll had kidnapped the twelve pet poodle puppies of Drabchester millionaire Sir Hugo Lightwater and was holding them to ransom. Susan was the ransom, becoming ten thousand counterfeit five pound notes, then changing back and helping Johnny Catbiscuit and Felix Pawson rescue the dogs. However, the pups also turned out to be counterfeits, cloned by Professor Troll. In another adventure, Dr Septic attempted to peel Susan from his fridge and write a shopping list on her. She has also been a stick-on tattoo on the arm of Fenella Fiendish and a carpet in Janice Evil's penthouse.

145

OTHER SUPERPOWERS

In her non-super life, Susan is the popular TV weather girl and quiz show hostess, Tina Winks. Tina is going out with trainee estate agent Julian House (24) aka Vest and Pants Lad. However, neither is aware of the other's super-identity. Tina lives in a flat (where else?) and enjoys limbo dancing and assembling flat-pack furniture.

PETS

A pet manta ray called Xeroxes, a moth called Tony, and some lichen called Barney, all of whom share her remarkable abilities, i.e. they're able to spread themselves completely flat and mimic their surroundings.

146

KERPOW!

THE ULTIMATE SUPERHERO'S HANDBOOK

SUPERHERO GADGETS, GIZMOS AND ESSENTIALS

PART ONE

SUPER-STUFF!

A MEMBER OF THE **SSSS** GROUP OF COMPANIES

JUST A SELECTION OF THE ASTOUNDINGLY STUNNING STUFF FROM OUR CURRENT CATALOGUE

AVAILABILITY ACCORDING TO SUPERHERO STATUS AND SECURITY CHECK

DISGUISE

MIRROR ME!™: Fool your adversaries into thinking you are them! Activate the tek-toggle on the velcro seal, spin round twice and you will look like them. This confuses them and prevents their hench-buddies from attacking

you for fear it's their master they're destroying.

PRICE: 10,000 R.H.

'I wouldn't go anywhere without mine!' **Hillman Avenger**

COPYFLAGE™: Looks just like an ordinary tube of sun lotion but strip off, slap it on and you instantly mimic your surroundings wherever you are! Desert, jungle, snowcapped peak, public library or lush green meadow. You simply disappear! Not to be used on outerwear.

PRICE: 600 R.H A TUBE.

'Even MY remarkable powers were enhanced by this superb product'!

Susan the Human-Post-It-Note

INTELLIGENCE

THE 'VERACITOR' PORTABLE LIE DETECTOR:

Talking to someone you suspect of being the enemy, or attempting to put you on a false trail or simply lying through their teeth? Well, wonder no more! This handy pocket lie detector will a) vibrate gently if it suspects the interviewee of being 'economical with the truth' b) throb energetically and emit a low beep if it thinks they're fibbing liberally and c) glow bright red, let out a warning siren scream and repeat, **'IT'S A LOAD OF PORKIES! A LOAD OF PORKIES!'** at 1,000 decidels as it recognises they're a double-dealing

149

dissembling pile of wombat droppings.

PRICE: 10,000 R.H. Batteries not included.

'Miraculous!' **Captain Unstoppable**

SURVIVAL

INSTANT-CROP: Suddenly find yourself starving in the Killer-Hurry desert, the wastelands of Snowberia, or a dungeon deep in the bowels of Septic Towers? Worry no more. This incredible garden on a roll will provide you with all the food you need until help arrives, or you figure a way out. All you have to do is unroll the bionically enhanced parchment, add a drop of water (or your spit), wait a

150

few minutes and, Abracadabra! you've got an instant crop of wholesome and nourishing organic vegetables.

Available in ten cropways including carrot, super-salad, sweet potato and midsummer medley. **PRICE: 750 RH A ROLL.**

'It got me out of a fix! And it's so healthy!' **Bodacious Babe**

FIRST AID KIT

LIMB-BOOSTERS™: Had your leg lopped off by a cutlass-wielding Robo-Goth, or your arm severed by a Sabre-Toothed Mule Man? Not a problem. Simply take two of these after meals, three times a day and hey presto your missing

part will have grown again, as good as new!
Sorted! Not recommended for under 5s.

PRICE: 5,000 HEROES FOR A PACKET OF 50.

'I swear by them!' **Danger Dude**

SKINCENTIVE™: Suffered a nasty flesh wound in a fight with an Icedrake? Just rub on some Skincentive Cream and your torn skin will regrow itself within minutes!

PRICE: 250 HEROES A TUBE. 10 TUBES FOR 2,000 HEROES.

'It really works!' **Vest and Pants Lad**

TRAINING

ZERO GRAVITY FLIGHT TRAINING TUBULE: It's a no-brainer! Almost every superhero can

152

fly. But where do they go to practise? Well with the ZGFTT you can practise your flight techniques and build up your stamina, all without leaving the comfort of your own home. Works just like a home jogging-machine but is fifty times more fun. All you do is get super-suited and superbooted, climb inside, flick the Gravity Obliterator, activate the Variable Wind Velocitor – and get flying. Only 12 metres by 6 metres by 4 metres but its possibilities are infinite! Can be erected in a jiffy!

PRiCE: 100,000

'I use mine every day! So useful for perfecting my legendary hovers and swoops!' **The Flying Fury**

EGMONT PRESS: ETHICAL PUBLISHING

Egmont Press is about turning writers into successful authors and children into passionate readers – producing books that enrich and entertain. As a responsible children's publisher, we go even further, considering the world in which our consumers are growing up.

Safety First
Naturally, all of our books meet legal safety requirements. But we go further than this; every book with play value is tested to the highest standards – if it fails, it's back to the drawing-board.

Made Fairly
We are working to ensure that the workers involved in our supply chain – the people that make our books – are treated with fairness and respect.

Responsible Forestry
We are committed to ensuring all our papers come from environmentally and socially responsible forest sources.

For more information, please visit our website at
www.egmont.co.uk/ethicalpublishing